A Fortune for Yo-Yo

The Richest Dog in the World!

Rose Impey
Shoo Rayner

ORCHARD BOOKS

ORCHARD BOOKS
96 Leonard Street, London EC2A 4XD
Orchard Books Australia
Unit 31/56 O'Riordan Street, Alexandria, NSW 2015
First published in Great Britain in 1994
This edition published in hardback in 2002
This edition published in paperback in 2003
Text © Rose Impey 1994
Illustrations © Shoo Rayner 2002
The rights of Rose Impey to be identified as the author
and Shoo Rayner as the illustrator of this work
have been asserted by them in accordance with the
Copyright, Designs and Patents Act, 1988.
A CIP catalogue record for this book is
available from the British Library.
ISBN 1 84121 874 X (hardback)
ISBN 1 84121 230 X (paperback)
1 3 5 7 9 10 8 6 4 2 (hardback)
1 3 5 7 9 10 8 6 4 2 (paperback)
Printed in Hong Kong.

1 84121 240 7

1 84121 238 5

1 84121 248 2

1 84121 256 3

1 84121 236 9

1 84121 246 6

1 84121 230 X

1 84121 234 2

1 84121 254 7

Read all the Colour CRACKERS books!

A Medal for **Poppy**
Colour CRACKERS
The Pluckiest Pig in the World!
Rose Impey and Shoo Rayner

1 84121 244 X

Too Many **Babies**
Colour CRACKERS
The Largest Litter in the World!
Rose Impey and Shoo Rayner

1 84121 242 3

Hot Dog **Harris**
Colour CRACKERS
The Smallest Dog in the World!
Rose Impey and Shoo Rayner

1 84121 232 6

Rhode Island **Roy**
Colour CRACKERS
The Roughest Rooster in the World!
Rose Impey and Shoo Rayner

1 84121 252 0

Welcome Home, **Barney**
Colour CRACKERS
The Loneliest Bat in the World!
Rose Impey and Shoo Rayner

1 84121 258 X

Pipe Down, **Prudle!**
Colour CRACKERS
The Most Talkative Parrot in the World!
Rose Impey and Shoo Rayner

1 84121 250 4

A Birthday for **Bluebell**
Colour CRACKERS
The Oldest Cow in the World!
Rose Impey and Shoo Rayner

1 84121 228 8

A Fortune for Yo-Yo

There are lots of rich *people*
in the world.
With swimming pools
and fast cars
and fancy aeroplanes.
But there aren't many rich *dogs.*
Well, not as rich as Yo-Yo.

Yo-Yo was a poodle.
A very handsome poodle.
He lived with Mrs Chumley-Lumley.
Mrs Chumley-Lumley lived
in London.

She lived with
Minchin, her butler,

and Minnie, her maid.

And Yo-Yo, of course.

Mrs Chumley-Lumley was very old.
Minnie was quite old too.
So was Minchin.
But Yo-Yo wasn't old.
He was quite young, actually, and
Mrs Chumley-Lumley spoiled him.

Minnie and Minchin looked after
Mrs Chumley-Lumley.
They waited on her
hand and foot.
They didn't mind.
That's what they were paid for.
But they *did* mind waiting on a dog!

Minnie and Minchin
didn't like Yo-Yo.

They didn't like having to
prepare his food

and feed him with a spoon.

They didn't like having to
take him for walks
and carry him there *and* back.

They didn't like Yo-Yo at all.
Mrs Chumley-Lumley did.
She loved him best in the world
and he loved her.

But Mrs Chumley-Lumley was old
and when she died
Minnie and Minchin couldn't wait
to get rid of Yo-Yo.
Poor Yo-Yo.

They thought to themselves,
"First we will get all
Mrs Chumley-Lumley's money,
then we will sell
that rotten dog."

But they were wrong.

In her will Mrs Chumley-Lumley
left fifteen million pounds.
She left it all to Yo-Yo.

She left Minnie
fifty pairs of shoes
and a hat.

She left Minchin a painting –
of herself.

But she left her money to Yo-Yo
because she loved him best of all.

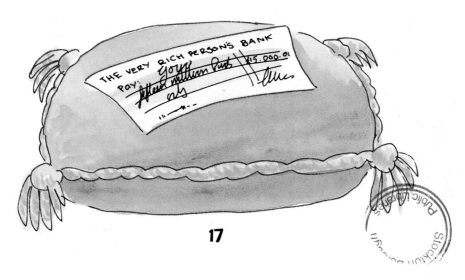

Minnie and Minchin were *furious.*

Fifteen million pounds – to a dog!
So they still had to wait on Yo-Yo,
if they wanted any wages.

Minnie and Minchin
wanted more than their wages.
They wanted to get their hands
on Mrs Chumley-Lumley's money.
What could they do?
Try to get rid of Yo-Yo,
of course!

They started to make plans.
This was their first plan:
sometimes, when
Mrs Chumley-Lumley
used to go on holiday,
Yo-Yo stayed at the kennels.

When she came home from holiday,
Minchin brought him back.

This time they would take Yo-Yo
to a different kennels.
This time they wouldn't
bring him back.

Clever plan, they thought.
So that's what they did.

But the lady at the kennels
recognised Yo-Yo.
She had seen his picture
in the papers.

She took him home in a taxi.

Yo-Yo stood at the door
and barked to be let in.

"I think you forgot your dog,"
said the lady.

Minnie and Minchin were *furious*.

"How kind,"
said Minnie.

"How lucky,"
said Minchin.

They gritted their teeth
and pretended to smile.
Yo-Yo gnashed *his* teeth.
He knew what they were up to.

The second plan they had
was this:
they would drive Yo-Yo
a very long way
into the country.

They they would take him
into a deep, dark wood,

tie him to a tree

and leave him there!

"Even better plan," they thought.
So that's what they did.

But Yo-Yo was cleverer
than they thought.
He snapped his lead.

He sniffed his way
out of the wood
and back to the road.

He stopped the traffic.
He got himself a ride home.

He stood at the door
and barked to be let in.

Minnie and Minchin were *furious.*

"We were so worried,"
lied Minnie.
"Thank goodness he's back,"
lied Minchin.

They both lied and smiled
at the same time.
But Yo-Yo wasn't fooled.

Their third plan was this:
they would take Yo-Yo
on a long train journey –
to the north of Scotland.
They would get off
at the first station.

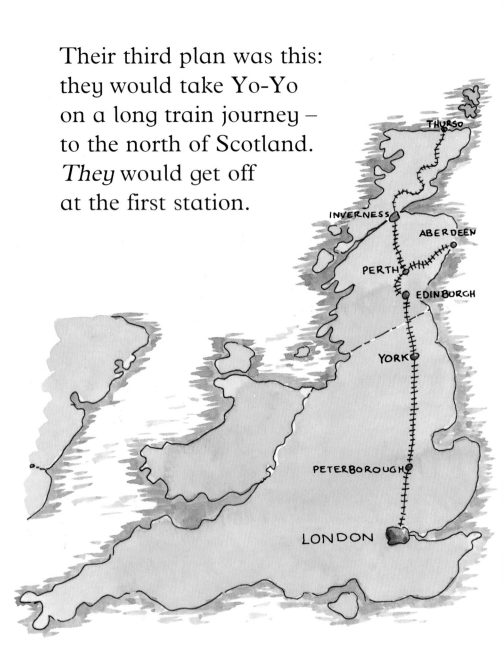

They would leave *him* on the train.

It would be the last
they would ever see of Yo-Yo.
"The best plan of all,"
thought Minnie and Minchin.
So that's what they did.

They left Yo-Yo sitting
on a seat
in a first class carriage.

But Yo-Yo was good at
making friends.
A kind family brought him back
on the next train.
Yo-Yo stood outside the door
and barked to be let in.

Minnie and Minchin were *furious*.

"How did it happen?"
said Minnie.
"Who would do such a thing?"
said Minchin.
They tried to look innocent.
They were not very good at it.

Minchin carefully closed the door.
"You'd think he was on
a piece of elastic," he said.
"Don't worry, we'll get rid of
him yet," said Minnie.

Yo-Yo gnashed his teeth
and demanded his dinner.
"If only dogs could talk,"
he thought.

Their last plan was
the most horrible plan of all.
Afterwards they were sorry
they had thought of it.
Very sorry indeed.

This was the plan:
they would wrap Yo-Yo up
in a parcel.

With lots of brown paper
and metres of string.

They would take the parcel
to the post office

and send it across the world –
to South America.

But Yo-Yo wasn't going to
put up with that quietly.
He started to bark.
Parcels don't usually bark.

When the customs men
opened it up
they were very surprised
to find a dog inside.

Yo-Yo had another ride home.
This time in a police car.

He stood at the door
and barked to be let in.
Minnie and Minchin were...

arrested!

Yo-Yo, the richest dog in the world,
lived in London.
He lived with Mitzi, his maid,
who was nothing like Minnie.

And Manners, his butler,
who was nothing like Minchin.

Every day he sat on his roof
garden eating and drinking
and having parties.

And Minnie and Minchin
went to prison.
They were...*so* sorry.

Crack-A-Joke

What kind of dog does
a hairdresser have?
A shampoodle!

What do you call two robbers?
A pair of knickers!

How do you know when it's been
raining cats and dogs?
**You keep stepping
in poodles!**

The poodle with oodles of jokes!

What do you get if you cross a cockerel with a poodle?
A cocker-poodle-doo!

Did you hear about the sheepdog trials?

They were all found guilty.

Look out, here comes the long arm of the paw!

It's wuff justice.

There are 16 Colour Crackers books. Collect them all!

❏ A Birthday for Bluebell	1 84121 228 8	£3.99
❏ A Fortune for Yo-Yo	1 84121 230 X	£3.99
❏ A Medal for Poppy	1 84121 244 X	£3.99
❏ Hot Dog Harris	1 84121 232 6	£3.99
❏ Long Live Roberto	1 84121 246 6	£3.99
❏ Open Wide, Wilbur	1 84121 248 2	£3.99
❏ Phew, Sidney!	1 84121 234 2	£3.99
❏ Pipe Down, Prudle!	1 84121 250 4	£3.99
❏ Precious Potter	1 84121 236 9	£3.99
❏ Rhode Island Roy	1 84121 252 0	£3.99
❏ Sleepy Sammy	1 84121 238 5	£3.99
❏ Stella's Staying Put	1 84121 254 7	£3.99
❏ Tiny Tim	1 84121 240 7	£3.99
❏ Too Many Babies	1 84121 242 3	£3.99
❏ We Want William!	1 84121 256 3	£3.99
❏ Welcome Home, Barney	1 84121 258 X	£3.99

Colour Crackers are available from all good bookshops,
or can be ordered direct from the publisher:
Orchard Books, PO BOX 29, Douglas IM99 1BQ
Credit card orders please telephone 01624 836000 or fax 01624 837033
or e-mail: bookshop@enterprise.net for details.
To order please quote title, author and ISBN and your full name and address.
Cheques and postal orders should be made payable to 'Bookpost plc'.
Postage and packing is FREE within the UK
(overseas customers should add £1.00 per book).
Prices and availability are subject to change.

1 84121 244 X

1 84121 240 7

1 84121 238 5

1 84121 252 0

1 84121 256 3

1 84121 236 9

1 84121 228 8

1 84121 230 X

1 84121 234 2

1 84121 248 2

1 84121 242 3

1 84121 232 6

1 84121 246 6

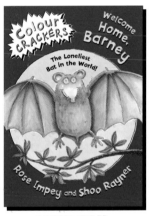

1 84121 258 X

1 84121 250 4

1 84121 254 7

Read all the Colour CRACKERS books!

Collect all the
Colour Crackers!